How do you explain cancer to a child?

That question was very much on my mind in the months after I was diagnosed with this disease.

At that time—it was October, 1987—my younger son Eric was only five. He could not understand what was happening to his mother and why his world was changing.

I wanted a simple and caring way to explain what causes cancer and why his mommy was in the hospital.

I felt the need to convince Eric and my other children—Caprice-Ann and Kurt—that life still goes on. It was important for them to know that it was alright to be happy even while I was sick.

These are some of the reasons why I wrote this book.

If you and your family have to face the difficult changes cancer makes in your lives, I hope our story will be of help to you.

Sincerely,

Carolyn Stearns Parkinson

For Eric Lee, Caprice-Ann, Kurt William
and any other child who
needs a special hug.

Text copyright © 1991 by Carolyn Stearns Parkinson
Illustrations copyright © 1991 by Elaine Verstraete
All rights reserved. No part of this book may be reproduced
or transmitted in any form or by any means, electronic or
mechanical, including photocopying, recording or by any
information storage and retrieval system, without permission
in writing from the Publisher.
Printed in U.S.A.

PARK PRESS P.O. Box 23205 Rochester, NY 14692-3205 (716) 381-1450
SAN 297-4940

Library of Congress Catalog Card Number: 91-062771
ISBN 0-9630287-0-7

MY MOMMY HAS CANCER

By Carolyn Stearns Parkinson
Illustrated by Elaine Verstraete

Carolyn Stearns Parkinson

PARK PRESS

Halloween is one of Eric's favorite times of the year, but this year it was different. He was getting his costume on to go "Trick or Treat" his mommy in the hospital.

As he dressed, Eric thought about the past week. It had been a very sad week.

Mommy had to go to the hospital to have an operation.

After the operation, people cried—his big brother Kurt, his sister Caprice-Ann, Daddy, Aunt Marilyn, Grandma, and even Grandpa.

Boy, was I scared for a while, thought Eric. I thought Mommy had died.

Then Daddy took me in his arms and told me Mommy had cancer. Cancer—that word sure made people sad but I didn't know why!

I asked Daddy what cancer was. He said cancer is a disease that makes people very sick.

He said our body is made up of many, many cells.

I didn't know what a cell was.

Daddy said that cells are like tiny, tiny
bubbles. These bubbles help us grow,
protect our body and keep us healthy.

Sometimes some bad bubbles appear. These bad bubbles grow very fast and "pop" or destroy the good bubbles.

Then you do not have enough good bubbles to keep you healthy.

In Mommy's case, Daddy said, those bad bubbles are called cancer cells.

I wanted to know why the word cancer made people cry. Daddy said that sometimes people die from cancer.

Daddy and I both had tears in our eyes and then I understood why that word made everyone so sad. I didn't want my mommy to die!

But Daddy said that Mommy was going to have chemotherapy. That means that she is going to get a lot of medicine. The medicine could make her feel sick or very tired for a while. But everyone hopes that the medicine will destroy the cancer cells and make them go away. Then Mommy will feel better.

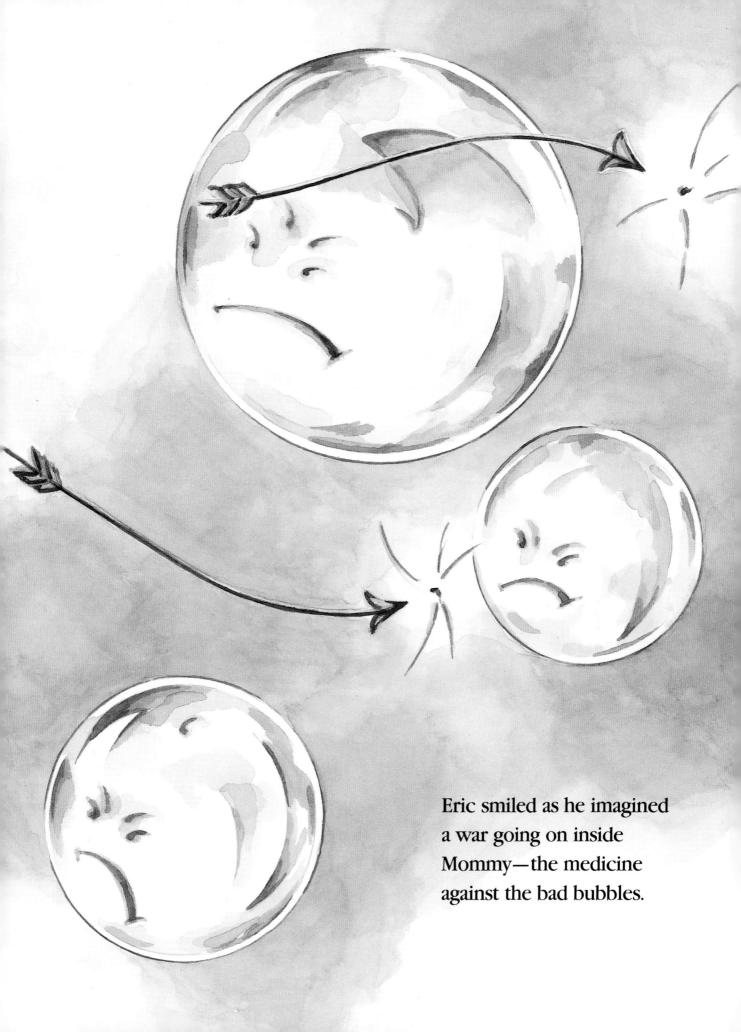

Eric smiled as he imagined
a war going on inside
Mommy—the medicine
against the bad bubbles.

Eric sat on his bed to put his sneakers on.

He remembered telling his Daddy that he just wanted his Mommy to come home and be like she was before she got sick.

Daddy said that she may never be like she was before. Everyone hoped that the chemotherapy would make her feel better for a long, long time. Then we could do many of the things we used to do.

Eric thought about the first time he went to see his Mommy in the hospital. She was in a bed with all kinds of tubes and stuff around her. It was a little scary.

When Mommy saw me, she started to cry. Mommy never cried very much. It made everyone cry. I was so sad that my stomach hurt.

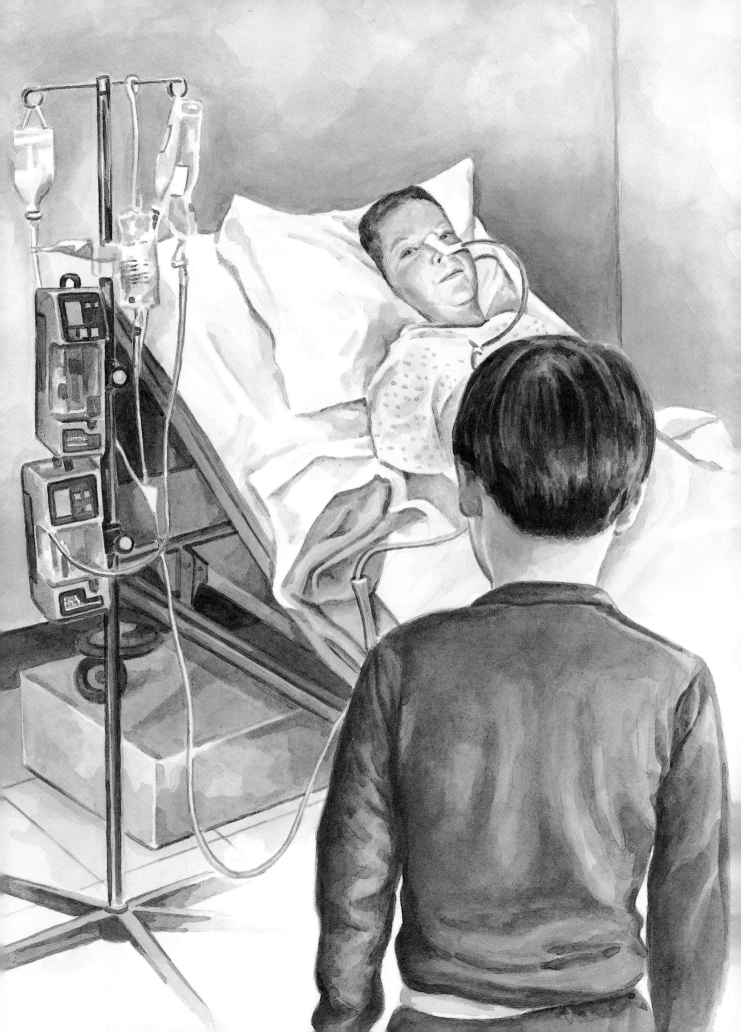

Eric quickly finished getting ready.
He was looking forward to seeing
his Mommy.

He wondered if she would have any treats
for him. After all, it was Halloween.

Eric walked quickly down the hall.
When he reached his Mommy's room,
he stopped and put on his mask.

He very quietly
peeked around the
door and said . . .

"Trick or Treat!"

I want to thank my family and all our new and "old" friends for their help and support in getting this book published.

I especially want to thank my husband, David, for always being there and having so much faith in me.

I wish to express a special Thank You to the following people and companies for their time, effort, special talents or financial assistance.

Arlene Sims, President, Signature Publications, Inc., Syracuse, NY
Economy Paper, Rochester, NY
Elaine Verstraete, Illustrator
Mr. & Mrs. Grover J. Stearns
Hank Shaw, The Guy with the Tie
Jones Chemicals, Inc., LeRoy, NY
Richard Harrington
Oncology Nursing Society
Seneca Paper, Rochester, NY
Upstate Litho, Michael A. Lehmann, President, Rochester, NY